Claire
· and the ·
Friendly Snakes

For James with love
L.T.

For Mom and Dad
J.D.F.

JP
TAT
c.1

Text copyright © 1993 by Lindsey Tate
Pictures copyright © 1993 by Jonathan Franklin
All rights reserved
Library of Congress catalog card number: 92-54642
Published simultaneously in Canada by HarperCollins*CanadaLtd*
Color separations by Hong Kong Scanner
Printed and bound in the United States of America
by Worzalla Publishing Co.
Designed by Martha Rago
First edition, 1993

$15,00   9-93

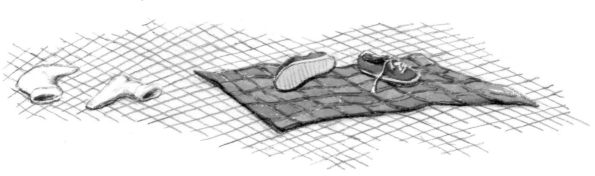

Claire
· and the ·
Friendly Snakes

Lindsey Tate · Pictures by Jonathan Franklin

Farrar · Straus · Giroux   **New York**

One Saturday morning when Claire was taking a bath she let out a high-pitched squeal.

"Soap in your eyes?" called Mom.

"Lost your towel?" boomed Dad.

"Snake!" shouted Claire. Then she giggled.

Coiled around the taps was a bright, silvery snake. What's more, it was spitting water at Claire.

Mom came running in. "You had me scared for a moment, Claire," she said, "but I think we can safely say this is a friendly snake."

"*Serpentinus amicalus*," added Dad, popping his head
around the door. He thought he was a whiz at Latin.

Later, Claire found Mom surrounded by mountains of material and spools of brightly colored thread. Mom was going to make a pair of trousers for Dad. She hated sewing. Dad hated the fact that all his trousers had shrunk in the washing machine.

"What are you up to, Claire?" asked Mom.
"I'm on a friendly-snake hunt," Claire announced.
Then she waved her hands in the air and shouted,
"Snake!"

Behind the sewing machine lay a long yellow
friendly snake. Dots, dashes, and numbers curled
down its back.

"Let's use the snake to measure Dad and
see how big to make his trousers," said Mom.

But there was too much tummy and not nearly enough friendly snake.

"Looks like we won't have to buy a new washing machine," said Mom with a smile.

"Not a very friendly snake," muttered Dad. "Claire, why don't you hunt for snakes somewhere else?"

"Snake!" yelled Claire, dancing up and down and pointing rudely.

A beautiful friendly snake, all butterflies and flowers, lay down the front of Dad's shirt.

"Perhaps," said Dad, pulling his tummy in and thrusting out his chest, "you could persuade your big brother, James, to wear one of these snakes at lunch."

Not James, thought Claire, heading toward his bedroom.

A handsome red friendly snake clambered, twisting
this way and that, up to James's ear. James was talking
to the friendly snake, and it was listening attentively.
Then James cupped his hand over the snake's ears
and shouted, "Claire, can't you see I'm busy?
Go and bother Grandma instead!"

What a good idea, thought Claire. "Snake!"
she hooted, leaping toward the ceiling.

A soft friendly snake of the palest pink was snuggled in Grandma's lap.

"Claire, dearie, could you help me wind the wool?" Grandma cooed, her knitting needles moving at quite a pace.

For a moment Claire considered; then something caught her eye.

A furry orange friendly snake
twitched enticingly.

"Oh!" said Claire, rushing to hug the snake.
"Mi-aa-o-oww!" yowled the cat, and she swished
her angry snake tail from side to side.

"What on earth are you doing, Claire?" asked Grandpa, peering down from watering his prize geraniums.
"Hunting for friendly snakes," replied Claire.

Then, in a much louder, Grandpa-scaring voice,
she shrieked, "Snake!"

A vivid green friendly snake nosed among the flowers, and streams of water shot forth from its mouth.

"Friendly-snake water is good for grubby hands, too," said Grandpa.

But Claire wasn't listening.

Just then Dad called "Lunchtime!" in a very hungry voice, and Mom said, "Say goodbye to the snakes now, Claire."

The water snake slept in a circle of soapsuds.

The measuring snake was curled up in a ball, exhausted after a morning of stretching.

The red listening snake
was quiet in a corner.

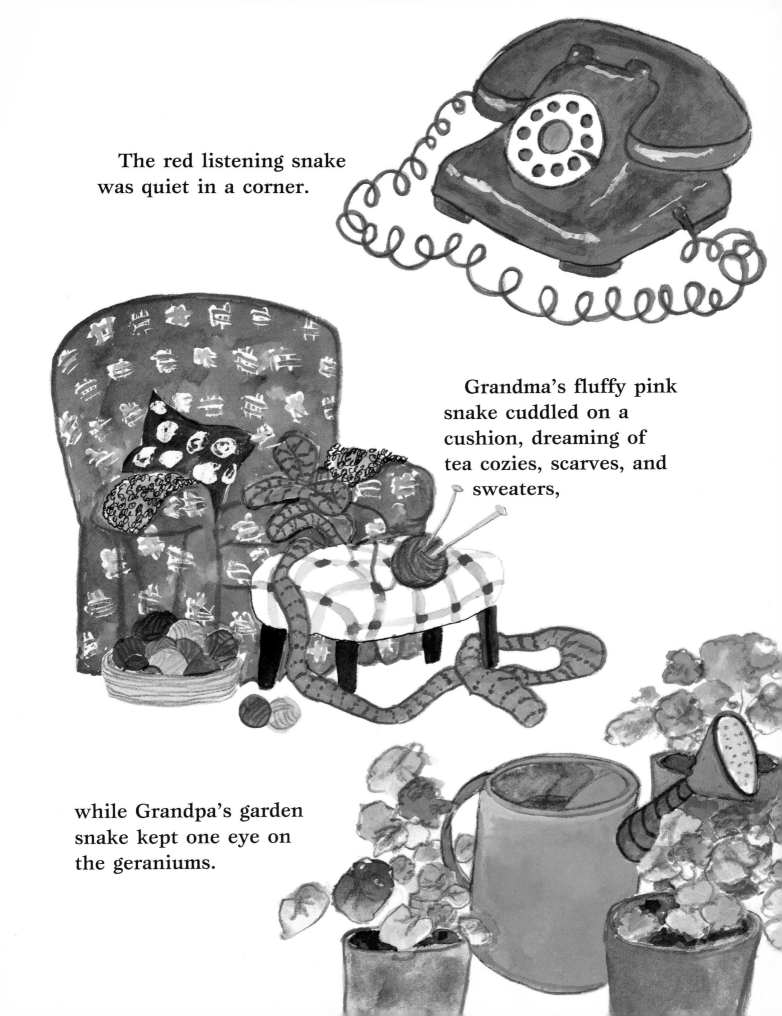

Grandma's fluffy pink
snake cuddled on a
cushion, dreaming of
tea cozies, scarves, and
sweaters,

while Grandpa's garden
snake kept one eye on
the geraniums.

The flowery snake was almost hidden under a large napkin, and the cat pulled her angry snake out of the way at Claire's approach.

"Let's say grace," suggested Dad, eyeing the food hungrily.

"Grace," said James.

"Snakes! Lots of them!" shouted Claire, knocking over her orange juice.

A bowl of thin spaghetti snakes wriggled steamily. "Oh, dear," said Mom, sighing. "Would anyone like some salad?"